Cora Semmes Ives

The Princess of the Moon

A Confederate fairy story

Cora Semmes Ives

The Princess of the Moon
A Confederate fairy story

ISBN/EAN: 9783337244071

Printed in Europe, USA, Canada, Australia, Japan

Cover: Foto ©Andreas Hilbeck / pixelio.de

More available books at **www.hansebooks.com**

THE

rincess of the Moo

A CONFEDERATE FAIRY STORY.

Written by a Lady of Warrenton, Va.

WARRENTON, VA.
1869.

TO THE

CHILDREN OF THE SOUTH,

WHO SUFFERED

DURING THE LATE WAR,

THIS LITTLE BOOK

IS DEDICATED.

INTRODUCTION

TO

The Princess of the Moon.

DEAR LITTLE SOUTHERN READERS:

WHEN we wish to amuse children, we create, in our imagination, a race of beings called "*Fairies*," and cause them to accomplish as many wonderful things as possible. This was my occupation, for the pleasure and happiness of my little ones, when sitting before a cheerful, hickory fire one chilly November evening.

It was a few months after the close of the war, and I was a guest at "Mecca,"* a beautiful Virginia home, (the

*In Warrenton.

war had deprived me of my **own,) and on** that evening my feelings **were** particularly sad from brooding over the **sufferings of** our dear Southern people, when my reveries were interrupted by a bevy of dear bare-footed little rebels. **who,** without ceremony, surrounded me and begged for a Fairy Story. **Of** course I **could not** resist their entreaties; so, after assuring them that, in reality, there exist no such creatures as Fairies, **I drew upon my** fancy for the following story.

Dear **children, we have** not a Fairy to watch over us, but a **Father in Heaven, who pities our sunny land, and** manifests **Himself to us in our afflictions.** He places us in a **"palace of purification," much more beautiful than** the one inhabited by **Randolph, for ours is this** bright world, filled **with furniture more dazzling** than any made by the hands of **man; the flowers, the birds,** the hills and vales; the silvery **streams, blue sky and glorious sun;** the stars, and that lustrous silver lamp, the **moon; —** what palace ever possessed such **Heavenly** ornaments **as these?** But let us remember that, with all its beauty, our world, like **Randolph's** prison, is only one of probation, to prepare and purify us for the eternal mansion, where the flowers will not fade, nor all that is bright and beautiful perish. Here we are to learn and practice virtue—which, like the Fairy's violets, will become jewels to adorn our crowns in Heaven. And when our Father wills that we should suffer through the wickedness of others, we must remember all the time that it is *He* who afflicts us, and then we shall feel less resentment against the *instruments* of His wrath.

I speak especially to you, little *sufferers* of the South, who during the war waged against us endured hunger and cold; were made homeless and fatherless. How well you remember that chilly night, when driven from your homes by brutal soldiers—the burning, the horrors which ensued;— you, poor little wanderers from Atlanta, and children of burning Columbia; you, starving ones, whose tears for bread broke many a widowed mother's heart; you, shivering ones, who watched the contents of your scanty wardrobes with

tearful eyes as they were torn and scattered to the winds and
flames. That Sunday frock! how you grasped the treasure
and begged it might be spared. Alas! the torch lighted and
consumed it even in the sanctuary of your arms. Ah! you
recollect all these scenes well—too well; but remember too,
dear children, it was *God* who willed it all. You, little son
of the brave papa, whose last words, on leaving for the war,
were: "Protect **thy mother and sisters, my boy." How**
bitter the torture that bound thee, hand and foot, whilst thy
sisters were **insulted and thy mother weeping.** Thou canst
not yet think that Heaven willed this. I see thee shake thy
head; thy **tears** of indignation return, **and thou feel'st in thy**
heart a desire for **revenge. Ah! it was a** cruel shock to thy
young nature, trained to chivalry from thy cradle. Let me
point thee to the only comfort left us. Turn thy gaze above
when **recalling that sorrow of the past; ever look up** to Him
who **permitted thy grief, and He will yet pour the** balm of
consolation into thy wounded soul.

But I will tire my little readers if I attempt to describe each one's sufferings. A record has already been made of them, and at the great day of *justice* the sorrows, as well as the crimes of every one, will be made manifest.

That the angels who watched over our brave land during the unequal struggle may have borne your tears and prayers to Heaven, where you will find them changed into bright crowns, is the heartfelt prayer offered for each one of you by

THE AUTHORESS.

PRINCESS OF THE MOON.

CHAPTER I.

IT was after the dreadful struggle between North and South that a poor Confederate soldier wandered in a wood near the ruins of his once splendid home.

He had been indulging his grief at the graves of his fond parents, recalling the proud day when he had buckled on his sword in defense of his native land, his mother's last embrace, his aged father's blessing, and his own promise to

return and brighten their declining years with
the laurels of victory and liberty.

But alas! how different from his sanguine
anticipation was the reality! And now, as he
thought of his bitter disappointment, and gazed
upon the blackened ruins of his once beautiful
home, deep anguish filled his heart. Raising
his tearful eyes Heavenward, the moon's pensive
rays fell upon his face with unusual brilliancy,
causing him to exclaim, "Ah! had I wings, how
gladly would I seek shelter on your distant,
peaceful shores, sweet moon." Instantly a
shadowy mist surrounded him, and through this
cloud he beheld a female of exquisite beauty.
A crescent of precious stones rested upon her
head, from which fell a long veil of silver gauze,

so completely enveloping her that he could only catch a glimpse of her robe beneath. This seemed to be of dark blue velvet, embroidered in jewels to represent stars.

"I am the Fairy of the Moon," said she, "and having witnessed your grief I desire to serve you. What would you have?"

The soldier fell upon his knees and promised to be her most faithful servant until death if she would only transport him to her dominions, as life in a conquered land had become to him a burden. The gentle Fairy smiled, and stamping her foot upon a rock, a beautiful white horse, magnificently caparisoned, immediately sprang forth.

"You will find every thing there for a long

journey," she said, pointing to the horse. "Make good use of the powers I give you, and you shall have my protection; but I warn you *not to fail* to return to this rock, on the first day of every month, to express your gratitude for my munificence. The name of your horse is *Hope*; and whenever you wish to ascend, descend, or stop on your journey, you have only to call "Hope." Should you, however, forget *me*, or neglect to visit me at this spot, you will in turn forget the name of your horse, and be unable to control his movements. In this I require the implicit obedience of those I serve. And now farewell; mount and leave this land which I have watched over in its prosperity, and now mourn over in its desolation. Yes, young man, I saw the torch applied to your home, and witnessed your noble father's last moments on the night he was turned, sick and suffering, from his own roof. I alone heard the blessings and last words he left for you. The next morning, when his body was found by his neighbors, they wondered that the dew upon his face and hair emitted the odor of violets: they knew not that I had wept over him, and the perfume of my tears never departs. Thus I became your father's mourner and your friend—and if you prove worthy I have many favors in store for you. Depart in peace." Saying this, she disappeared in the same shadowy mist which at first surrounded her.

Randolph (for this was the soldier's name) inspected his noble steed, finding a pair of snow

white wings under his flowing mane, and pro-
visions and clothing stored in golden cases under
the saddle. He immediately mounted and exclaimed, "Hope!" when, to his delight, the
wings gracefully spread themselves, and he
found himself flying rapidly through the air;
and what was most remarkable, he possessed the
power of seeing through space into the interior
of the houses and cities he passed. Day was
now breaking, and he frequently called Hope to
stop, that he might enjoy the views of the different countries and beautiful cities over which he
hovered; and sometimes he descended to take a
closer view of the interior. His own desolate
land he could not gaze upon without tears, for
he beheld misery and want in all directions.

He saw the twenty thousand that had been driven from one fair city, living in stables, barns, &c. &c.; and some even without this poor shelter;* another twenty thousand dwelling among the blackened ruins of their once beauteous town—the Eden of Carolina.†

Then he viewed the homes of the conquerors, abounding in plenty, and decked in the spoils they had so cruelly acquired. The sight had such a sickening effect, particularly as in one place he found his own old family plate adorning a festive board, that his senses became confused —and but for the outstretched wings of Hope he would have fallen. On recovering himself, he determined to continue his upward course,

*Atlanta.　　　　†Columbia.

2

without further delay—and he commanded Hope
to bear him at once to his destination, and in a
short time he arrived safely in the moon. He
then alighted and commenced to survey his new
home. The air surrounding this new world had
upon him a most transporting effect—it being
soft, and yet exhilarating: the zephyrs made the
most delightful music as they fanned the luxu-
riant foliage, while gentle showers, imparting
the odor of attar-of-roses, constantly moistened
the earth. The flowers were the rarest and the
birds the brightest he had ever seen. There
was no night in this sublime region. He soon
discovered signs of habitation; and the unpre-
tending cottage, as well as the palatial residence,
gave evidence of a happiness and peace which
was remarkable.

After wandering many days he approached a magnificent palace, which, from its size and grandeur, he knew must be inhabited by the King; for he had learned, on conversing with the people, that a King reigned over them who was both wise and good.

The castle excelled anything he had ever seen. It was of singular and graceful architecture, particularly the innumerable towers that surrounded it; and from whose lofty summits floated the silvery banner of the moon. Knowing he could not enter without a special invitation from the King, he did not seek admittance into the palace; but, making use of Hope's wings, he alighted in a secluded grotto within the walls surrounding the royal grounds. He

spent several hours in examining this wonderful
spot, filled with beautiful ponds, lakes, woods
and meadows. Verdant groves were traced by
silver streams, over which floated enchanted gon-
dolas of every form and description. The aged
and children formed the pleasure parties of these
happy excursions, and once a week they were
permitted this privilege.

Randolph was struck with their kind and
pleasing manners, and on conversing, discovered
that such was the peace and content of these
people, that they had never heard of *war*, and
knew nothing of its meaning. His satisfaction
was unbounded at the thought that he was at
last in a country which would never be conquered, or even invaded—that the people were

free and happy—their good King seeming like
a loving father. He was also informed of the
existence of the King's daughter—a princess of
marvelous beauty; and an intense longing and
determination to see her possessed him. As the
grounds were many miles in extent he had no
difficulty in concealing Hope, and keeping at a
distance from the castle. At last he became
tired, and was just about to throw himself upon
the soft, bright turf, when he caught a glimpse
of what seemed an *angel's dream*—it was too
beautiful for reality, and he was so transfixed
with admiration that he had no power to move,
and consequently was unable to avoid being
seen by the lovely creature who approached
him. On beholding him, her face became suf-

fused with blushes, and she was about to retreat
—but turning towards him, as with a sudden
thought, she exclaimed: "Should you be seen
here, your death is inevitable; such must be the
fate of any of your sex who look upon me before
my marriage, except the one destined by my
grand-mother to be my husband. He is to
appear on my eighteenth birth-day, but until
then I am as one dead to the world."

"Lovely princess," Randolph replied, "I am
a wanderer from a distant world, and a stranger
here, but a good Fairy watches over and protects
me: so you need not fear. I beg that you will
let me have the happiness of sometimes beholding
you." She assured him it would be impossible,
and urged his instant flight, as they were at that

moment in the greatest danger of being seen by her grand-mother. However, he persisted that his friend who had sent him to the moon would guard them both from harm, and he implored her not to banish him from her charming society. Then, to touch her heart, he told her the history of his life—describing the once happy and prosperous land of his birth; then the misery and ruin brought upon his beloved people by a dreadful war; last of all, his own despoiled home, and his meeting with the good Fairy who had taken pity on him. But he did not tell how she had transported him to this place, for he felt he ought not to divulge this secret without first consulting his benefactress.

On concluding the sad narrative he discovered

the cheeks of the princess were wet with tears, whereupon he again entreated to see her occasionally, but she only shook her head in disapproval, and replied: that as it would certainly endanger his life, it was best for them to part— she only wished they had never met, as she feared even now it might occasion his ruin.

In token of farewell she gave him her hand, which he fervently kissed, and then glided away in the direction she had come, leaving Randolph in distress and despair. He was now alone with Hope, who gazed at him in mute sympathy, and then this trusty friend outstretched his wings, as if inviting his master to mount; and on his doing so, carried him far out of sight of the "Castle of Rest," as the king's palace was called.

CHAPTER II.

THE gentle motions of his horse lulled our hero into a peaceful sleep, and on awaking he found himself approaching a gate of surpassing beauty, and apparently of massive silver. Feeling curious to know what lay beyond, he ordered Hope to halt while he tried to gain admittance. He could not open the gate, but through a small crevice he perceived an angel with a drawn sword, on which was inscribed, in letters of fire, the word "Paradise." The slight glimpse he had of the interior of this exquisite spot, and the remembrance of the misfortunes that had been brought upon him and the world by the disobedience of those first parents for whose happiness so much beauty had been created, filled him with sadness, but reminded him of his good benefactress, who required him to return to express his gratitude at the beginning of each month.

He suddenly remembered that he had scarcely time to make the contemplated journey, and for the first time he felt glad that the princess had not permitted him to remain longer in her presence, as he might have forgotten the good Fairy's injunction until it was too late. He now commanded Hope to bear him in all haste to the appointed rendezvous.

Many beautiful countries and enticing scenes attracted his gaze, but he resisted the temptation to stop and admire, lest in the enjoyment of his own pleasures, he should forget the Fairy's command. Finally the picture of his own sad land was again in sight, but he dared not linger as he had only a few moments left in which to reach the enchanted rock. As he drew near he beheld his kind friend awaiting him. She greeted him joyfully, for her delight that he had come in time, was very great. "I would rather bless than afflict you," she exclaimed, "therefore in future do not risk my displeasure; partake of the pleasures I allow you *in moderation,* and you will never forget to return on the appointed day."

Saying this, she motioned him to a rustic seat near by, and threw back her silver veil, when a pair of lustrous, mistful, dark eyes beamed upon him with gentle kindness. "My object in summoning you here" she said, "is not only to exact obedience, but also to bestow upon you still greater favors." Randolph gazed fondly upon his benefactress, and promised to return, in future, a day or two *before* the appointed time, and thus avoid all risk of delay. The fairy then raised her wand, and immediately a beautiful, clear lake sprang forth at their feet. Its waters, like a mirror, reflected the enchanted bower of the moon in which Randolph had met the princess. He now beheld her again standing near the spot where they had parted. Her face was pale and

sad. She approached the tree against which he
had leaned when talking to her, and to his
delight he saw her imprint a kiss upon the rough
bark. By this he knew she was thinking of
him. But what was his astonishment to behold
at the same moment the part her sweet lips had
touched fall from the tree, and in its place a
golden case appear containing a likeness of himself! And now he knew how he was beloved
by witnessing the joy of his adored princess.
Unconscious that his gaze was upon her, she
poured forth her feelings in tears of joy, pressed
the picture to her lips, and then placed it near
her heart. This sight filled him with such happiness that he was on the point of mounting
Hope and flying to the moon, when the Fairy's

sweet voice again arrested his attention. "Be cautious" she said, "how you intrude upon the solitude to which her grand-mother has condemned her. Had any other young man presented himself in the enchanted bower as you have done, he would have been punished with instant death; but I watched over and saved you. That lovely creature is destined for a husband of her grand-mother's choice. It is my desire that you should be selected, and I will assist you on condition you continue to obey my order, by returning at the appointed time, to this place to express your thanks. But remember that punishment awaits those who disobey me."

Transported with delight at the idea of again

meeting the princess, and of being able to assure her of the protection of the Fairy, he fell at the feet of his friend, and whilst he was pouring forth his gratitude in the most affectionate terms, she disappeared. Mounting his faithful steed, Randolph was, in an incredibly short time, carried to a thick wood near the enchanted bower of the Palace of Rest. Concealing Hope, he proceeded on foot to find the princess. Unconscious of his presence, she was sighing and grieving as she sadly gazed upon the likeness clasped in her hands; but when she saw her lover in person at her feet, her whole countenance became transformed. It was like the sun breaking through the clouds on a rainy day. Her golden curls fell in graceful profusion over her neck and shoulders; her soft brown eyes, a moment before so mournful, now beamed upon him with bewitching light; her ruby lips wreathed in enchanting smiles around teeth that rivaled the rarest pearl; while her pale cheeks became instantly suffused with the tint of the rarest rose.

Randolph, unable to resist such charms, immediately gave expression to the devotion he felt, and declared he could not survive separation from her. He then told her of his visit to the good Fairy, and of the protection she had promised them, and begged the princess to return his love without fear. It was impossible to resist such entreaties, and the princess by her drooping eyes and blushing cheeks confessed what her timid lips could scarcely utter. And now this happy pair passed several hours of each day in sweet communion with each other, rambling through the groves and shades of the Palace of Rest. But Randolph became impatient to have his fate decided, so he determined on an expedient. He learned that the king had a great passion for music, and that aged musicians were permitted to enter the palace when all others of the sex were excluded. Now Randolph was a proficient in this accomplishment, so he procured a white wig, and having completely disguised his face, presented himself at the palace and was without difficulty admitted into the presence of the king. This imposing monarch sat on a throne of gold inlaid with

precious stones, and though *pride* was marked
upon his noble countenance, it was softened by
an expression of kindness and benevolence.

The queen and their daughter were also
present, and when Randolph gazed upon his
adored princess, the effect of her resplendent
charms was almost too great for his presence of
mind. He dared not trust himself to look a
second time, lest he should be unable to exer
cise his musical powers for the pleasure of the king.
He commenced at once, and having finished
his first efforts, he noticed that the king seemed
much gratified, and to the great delight of our
disguised troubadour, desired to speak with him.
He made many inquiries of his name, country,
destination, &c., and seeming much interested,

Randolph determined to give him a portion of his history, concealing of course the means used by the Fairy to transport him to the moon.

The king was very just, and when he had heard from Randolph of the terrible war in which his countrymen had been engaged, of the many sufferings they had endured before being overpowered by countless hordes of a meddling, peddling race, called "Yankees," his face darkened with indignation. "Remain in my palace," said he to Randolph, "I should like to know more of your poor, stricken land. You shall become one of my household, and teach the princess your beautiful accomplish-ment, in which you excel any one I have ever heard in my own land." Randolph was almost overcome with delight, and the agitation of his feelings added much to the pathos and tenderness of his next song—"The Conquered Banner." When he had finished it, the eyes of even the stern old king were glistening with tears, and the princess was obliged to leave the room.

CHAPTER III.

AND now Randolph was established at the castle as one of the household, and when not engaged with the king, or teaching and making love to the princess, he amused himself inspecting the interior of this grand and wonderful structure. It excelled his most brilliant expectations, being a little world within itself, and evidently not built by the hands of man. Discovering that all this grandeur was the work of a powerful fairy who presided over the destiny of his household, he understood why it was that the king obeyed so implicitly the grand-mother's injunctions regarding the princess. In his moments of solitude his heart failed, lest he should be discovered and banished from the society of his beloved, but the remembrance of his own good Fairy's promise encouraged and reassured him.

It is impossible to imagine the magnificence, taste and comfort presented to Randolph as he wandered through this grand old castle.

The entrance hall was a mile in circumference, and in its centre a fountain sent forth, with sparkling jets of water, delightful music—which on the arrival of guests, would be gay and rejoicing, but sad and mournful on their departure. Statues made of rare and wonderful stone and metal were arranged in graceful groups, and represented the virtues most admired by the king. In this hall the walls were of azure, bespangled with stars of silver, and the ceiling was a magnificent picture of the joys of heaven. Delicious perfumes **were** constantly sprinkled by invisible hands, and the **floors** seemed to reflect, as a mirror, exquisite flowers of every shape and hue. Doors around the hall opened into the various apartments, too numerous and beautiful to describe. On **one** side a balcony overlooked the "Grotto of Silence," whose refreshing shades were never disturbed by any **one** but the king himself.

As it would fill volumes to give an accurate description of this enchanted palace, which surpassed anything ever seen or heard of, I will now continue my story and relate how our friend Randolph, in the enjoyment of his pleasures, lost all recollection of his kind benefactress. The day arrived for their meeting, but the Fairy waited in vain at the appointed spot until, unable to restrain her impatience, she touched the rock with her wand, and the lake again appeared, in which was reflected the Castle of Rest. Seated by the side of the princess, Randolph was apparently forgetful of everything save his own happiness. He was at that moment singing one of his sweetest songs, and the princess was gazing sadly upon him, for she knew that the time was fast approaching when they must part forever, as her grand-

mother's favorite was to appear on her **eighteenth**
birth-day, which was close at hand. Notwith-
standing the apparent difficulties, our hero had
determined to act the honorable part of informing
the king of his true age and circumstances,
trusting to his good Fairy's promises, and the
affection he knew the king entertained for him.
Sadly the gentle Fairy surveyed the picture in
the crystal lake, and commenced to weep, for
she well knew that Randolph's forgetfulness of
herself would bring trouble upon the happy
pair, in spite of her affection for them. "Ah!"
thought she, "if he would only come to me all
would yet be right, and my poor grand-daughter
saved much sorrow." (The reader has no doubt
surmised that *Randolph's good Fairy and the*

princess' grand-mother were one and the same.)
She mourned and grieved in vain, for Randolph
was oblivious of everything but the princess.
At last day dawned and she departed, leaving
the ground wet with her tears, from which
sprang a bed of fragrant violets.

In the meanwhile Randolph opened his heart
to the good old king, told his unbounded love
for his daughter, and the deception it had driven
him to practice, and how the promises of the
Fairy had encouraged him to hope for success.
But as dearly as the king loved him, he dared
not disobey the wishes of the grand-mother, and
with sad heart he gave orders that his favorite
musician should die at sunset, and for the *first*
time sorrow and distress reigned throughout the
Castle of Rest.

The grief of the poor princess was so great that her life was despaired of. Randolph preferred death to separation from her, and therefore came forth with seeming cheerfulness, at the appointed hour, to the place of execution.

CHAPTER IV.

RANDOLDPH'S only request was to bid farewell to Hope, and as no one knew the secret connected with the horse, his desire was gratified. He embraced his faithful steed, and speaking to him as to a friend, he begged him to remain with his beloved princess, and to be to her the trusty friend he had always been to him. The scene was so touching that there was a murmur of sympathy through the crowd. Suddenly Randolph perceived a gleam of encouragement in Hope's eyes, and he exclaimed imploringly to the king, "Permit me, sire, to take a farewell ride on my beloved horse in your presence, in front of the Castle." The king consented, and when Randolph had mounted he called in a loud voice "Hope," when to the amazement of all present, white wings appeared and he was borne with the swiftness of an arrow high into the air. His cloak and wig fell at the same instant at the feet of the king, who in wonder and astonishment gazed at the handsome youth, and then with a joyful countenance exclaimed, "my good people, I have just discovered that our friend is the youth intended by the Fairy as the husband of my daughter. Fool that I was, not to make him cast aside his disguise before I

passed sentence upon him, for the Fairy gave
me a picture to enable me to recognize my intended son-in-law. Alas! I fear my oversight
will bring upon all of us her indignation." Then
he ordered his people to call out to Randolph
that he should not die, but to return and marry
the princess. Though Randolph heard their
cries and seemed to understand them he
continued to rise higher and higher until he
altogether disappeared. By this the king
knew that his want of discretion had offended
the Fairy, and he mournfully repaired to the
Grotto of Silence, where no one dared follow.
It was in this place that the grand-mother
always met him when she wished to communi-
cate her wishes, and on this occasion he found

her with displeasure marked upon her countenance. "I deserve your condemnation for my unjust sentence," he exclaimed, "but let my desire of *implicit obedience* to your command, plead my cause." "Oh! king," she replied, "let this sad lesson teach you never to be hasty in your judgments, as appearances too often deceive even the wisest and best. You should have sought assistance and light from me to guide you in this important matter." So saying, she left him to reflect on the sad occurrences of the day.

To return to Randolph. I have said that he heard and understood the cries of the people, and knew that the king had relented and determined to allow him to marry his daughter, so

he resolved to descend at once, but to his
amazement he could not *think of*, much less *call*
the name of his horse. Suddenly the Fairy's
command and threat flashed across his mind,
and knowing that the time for their meeting had
passed, he felt that he must suffer the fatal con-
sequences of his neglect. Grief and remorse at
his forgetfulness of so good a friend, overcame
him to such a degree that he fell into a swoon
which lasted two days.

On recovering, he found himself still swiftly
ascending and passing by innumerable beautiful
worlds without even the comfort of enjoying the
pictures they presented—for the power of calling
Hope was still denied him. At last he saw in
the distance a magnificent gate, resting on

clouds of azure, tipped with gold. Above this gate, in glittering letters, formed of precious stones, appeared the word HEAVEN, around which bright angels were hovering and making music with their wings. Hope could proceed no further, and Randolph's grief was only increased at thus finding himself just *outside* of the gate of Heaven, with no power to enter.

Soon an angel of surpassing beauty approached, bearing in its arms the soul of an infant. Many other angelic spirits followed in quick succession, in company with bright, purified souls, about to enter Heaven. Randolph could read in their faces the joy of the guardian angels, that the precious souls entrusted to their care had been by them safely conducted through

4

a world of snares, and were now going to enjoy
the delights of eternal happiness.

The jeweled gate soon opened to receive the
numerous throng, and there issued forth music
so exquisite, and a light so brilliant, that Randolph was thrown into an ecstasy which ren-
dered him insensible. In this state he would
have fallen into space but for the outstretched
wings of Hope, ever ready to sustain him.
When he became conscious, Heaven's delicious
melody still resounded in his ears; but the gate
being half closed, the full light no longer blinded
him, and he was able to catch a glimpse of the
angel who guarded the entrance of this blessed
abode. **This** bright spirit seemed arrayed in
rainbows, and a halo of glory surrounded its

head. It bore a crown in its hand, as if waiting to bestow it upon an expected soul. Across its breast was a sash of sunbeams, on which was inscribed in golden letters the word "Hope." At this sight Randolph was transported with joy, and calling on Hope with all the strength of his voice, he immediately began to descend.

After traveling through the air for many days he perceived the welcome glimmer of the moon's silver beams. But he dared not stop without having first visited the enchanted rock; for, though he had, of course, lost all reckoning of time, still he determined to atone, as much as possible, for his former neglect, by hastening immediately to the appointed place. He hovered for an instant over the Castle of Rest, and his resolution *not to delay* nearly forsook him as he beheld, reclining in the enchanted bower, his adored princess, apparently dying. He lingered one instant, and was just about to risk everything and fly to her side, when he saw an entreating tear in the eye of his faithful Hope. By this sign he knew that if he stopped, even for a short space of time, he would be too late for his appointment with the Fairy; so with an aching heart he commanded Hope to fly with him from temptation.

At the same moment the good Fairy was watching his movements in the Lake of Reflection. During his struggle between *inclination* and *duty*, she closed her eyes, as if unwilling either to gaze upon his sufferings, or to witness his unfaithfulness to her commands—knowing well that a second disregard of her wishes would cause him forever to lose her care and protection. In a few moments he appeared in her presence, and unable longer to endure his sufferings, he fell fainting at her feet. Plucking the violets which her tears, at his former neglect, had occasioned, she sprinkled them over his prostrate form, and immediately a blush and smile overspread his pale features. But before he opened his eyes she mounted Hope and flew away, leaving him alone beside the Lake of Reflection. On awakening, as if from a horrid dream, he recognized the Fairy's rendezvous, and realized at once the full extent of his misfortunes. Finding himself covered with fragrant **violets, which he knew were the** tears of his benefactress, he gathered, and kissing them, placed these tokens of her love near his heart, determining never to part with them. At that moment he beheld the Lake of Reflection, in which was pictured the Castle of Rest, **and, to** his surprise, saw the Fairy borne within its enclosure on his beloved Hope. Now, that his faithful horse was gone, he had nothing left to remind him of his good Fairy but the violets and the lake. Gazing into the crystal waters he beheld with astonishment **the** Fairy, seated by the side of the princess, uttering words which seemed at once to restore the latter to life and happiness. Then there seemed great rejoicing in the moon. The great doors of the castle were opened, and throngs came forth to do honor to the **Fairy**—who, **to** Randolph's amazement, was welcomed and embraced by the king with the utmost affection.

At this moment the lake disappeared, and there stood in its place a beautiful house and grounds, which Randolph found, on examination, to be provided with every comfort **and** luxury; but he himself was deprived of all sense of enjoyment. As soon as he possessed himself of what he desired to have, it assumed the shape of something distasteful to him. Flowers, when gathered by him, turned into thorns; wine into water; and every delicacy, when touched, became bread; thus forcing him to become satisfied with this simple diet. The house was inhabited by people who appeared, from a distance, to be most charming and agreeable; but whenever Randolph approached them, they became so hideous and disgusting that he shrank away into a solitude which forced him to gaze upon all that **was** delightful without the privilege of enjoying anything.

In this place he spent his time until the day again approached for his meeting with the Fairy. In the meanwhile the bouquet of violets grew less and less. Each day one would disappear, and he would find in its place, inscribed in **letters** of diamonds, on a golden scroll, the name of **some** virtue—first, *Patience*, then *Charity, Humility*, **Perseverance**, &c., until there was but one violet left. On the eve of the day he was to meet the Fairy, that also disappeared, and in its place he found a miniature of his kind friend, under which was written *Gratitude.* Touching a spring in the golden case, a picture of the lovely princess was disclosed, under which was inscribed the word *Love.* He now felt convinced that his troubles were coming to an end, and that his beloved princess would be the reward of the virtues he had learned to practice in this singular place of banishment.

CHAPTER V.

T last the long looked for day arrived, and he hastened to meet the Fairy, who soon appeared, and, embracing him with joyful affection, commanded him to mount Hope and ascend to the moon, where the king and his daughter and all the inhabitants were awaiting him with impatience. "In fact," she exclaimed, "I am the grand-mother of the princess, and long ago destined you for her husband. This happiness would have been yours on her eighteenth birth-day had you not disobeyed my wishes, thus forcing me to condemn you to the Castle of Purification. Now you are worthy to become a subject of our sinless dominion, having been purified from all stains of earth." A touch of her wand changed the sombre apparel he had worn during the days of his probation into a magnificent Confederate uniform. He then mounted Hope, and in a wonderfully short time found himself in the moon.

The instant he appeared he was greeted with the most melodious music, and crowds followed him to the Palace of Rest. Randolph's heart beat with rapture when the gates were opened, and the king came forth to meet him, "Come, my son, thy bride awaits thee."

In the festal hall stood the princess, radiantly

beautiful. A veil of snowy gossamer, spangled
with tiny diamonds, enveloped but did not con-
ceal her lovely face. Upon her brow rested a
wreath of pearls, set in the form of lilies, and
her dress of richest satin fell in flowing folds
around her graceful form. Lovingly, though
timidly, she stepped forward to meet him—but
language fails me in portraying joy like theirs.

After receiving the blessing of the king and
queen, they were proclaimed "man and wife."
Thousands of trumpets sounded forth the joyful
event, in the midst of which they were led to
the throne prepared for them.

As they were receiving the congratulations of
the people, the festivities were suddenly suspended by an unexpected event which struck

terror into the hearts of all beholders. Hovering over the castle were several most singular looking objects, which in a short time descended to the ground. From these curiously shaped affairs floated banners of red and white stripes, and in a few minutes a number of individuals issued forth, carrying *"carpet-bags"* and *"traps"* of all descriptions. Congratulating themselves upon their good luck in discovering a new country, which they *"guessed"* was going to surpass "the best government the world ever saw," they set to work at once, and commenced a survey of the place. The new-comers seemed not the least disconcerted by the crowd of peaceful-looking people who gazed so wonderingly and calmly upon them. Indeed, they made themselves so much at home, that to a casual observer they would have appeared to be the owners of this fair country and the natives seemed the intruders. The sudden cessation of the music and rejoicing reached the hall where Randolph and his bride, unconscious of what was taking place outside, were receiving the congratulations and toasts of his friends as the honored Confederate, the adopted Prince, and the future King of the Moon. In a few minutes the death-like stillness outside was explained, as the uninvited guests appeared in the festal hall. But when they saw a handsome Confederate soldier seated on a throne by the side of his beautiful bride, and the magnificence and pomp surrounding him, for the first time they halted and even looked a little abashed.

At this moment one of the party, whose grimaces and contortions had occasioned general terror, especially among the children, rushed forward, exclaiming: "God bless me! if here aint Massa at last, 'live and well arter all!" This individual was of entirely a different appearance from the rest of the party—his skin being black and his head woolly—and as he rushed frantically towards Randolph, whom he seized in his arms, the poor princess became so alarmed that she fell into a swoon, causing for awhile great confusion and dismay. Meantime the guests whose presence had caused such consternation, made themselves perfectly at home; but the people, perceiving that the woolly head appeared to be a friend of their new prince, restrained

their impatience until he should explain the
meaning of what they saw. He rose from his
throne and addressed them thus: "My illustrious
king and father; my beloved adopted citizens—
this singular individual (pointing to the grinning
darkey) was an old and trusty servant belonging
to my father's household, and one to whom I
am greatly attached. He heard that an expedi-
tion was forming to survey the moon, and having
dreamed that he should find me here, he was
induced to join the party in hopes of realizing
his wishes. After setting out, he discovered
that the adventurers were the very persons who
had burned down and driven from my home my
aged parents." At this moment the exploring
party commenced to run, dropping in their haste

their carpet-bags, from which fell numerous valuable articles—"*spoons*" predominating. The good old darkey clapped his hands delightedly, crying, "hurrah! Massa! dem's yourn. I seed um steal um, but dar'nt say a word. Poor old Massa! God bress him—was a dying, and no one but me to take him out of the flames!"*

The surveyors reached their *balloons* (their means of conveyance) without molestation, for as I have before said, the people of the moon were a peaceful race, and the Fairy alone exercised the prerogative of justice. She stood there awaiting them, her face glowing with indignation as she exclaimed: "Ah! I have caught you

---

*In Selma, during the late war, an old man was burned to death in his own house by Yankee soldiers, no faithful darkey being near to rescue him from the flames.

at last, demons of cruelty, and I have now the power to punish you, which I had not outside of my own dominions." Touching the balloons with her wand, they were instantly transformed into hideous dragons, which at once surrounded their unhappy victims. Then she summoned Randolph to appear and pronounce sentence upon them; but this noble youth, who had learned, in the Palace of Purification, to know and love virtue, begged her, in honor of his wedding day, to release them, saying, "Beloved benefactress, did you not forgive me my base ingratitude? Permit me, then, to restrain my vengeance, even though these enemies have driven me from my home and deprived me of every earthly consolation. Through the sorrow they have brought on me, I have learned *Charity*, whose sublime lessons are only taught in the school of adversity. It is there we learn that life would become insupportable if fellow-creatures do not assist and encourage each other. Behold," he continued, his face beaming with love, "my mother's gentle spirit pleads for these sinners;" and he held up to their view a miniature, under the lovely face of which, formed in letters of precious stones, were these words:— "Blessed are the merciful, for they shall obtain mercy." "This is a valued tribute, presented my father by the citizens of my native town in gratitude for his *charity* during a terrible pestilence, when he and my pious mother opened their doors, their hearts and their purses to the suffering. I found this priceless relic just now among the ill-gotten goods dropped so hurriedly by the intruders. It is prized above all treasures, and comes to bless my wedding-day, and give the poor Confederate soldier a suitable offering for his bride." Turning towards her, and throwing the chain around her neck, he softly whispered, "Accept, beloved one, this my only possession, but it is worthy even of a princess, **for** it is my mother's **face** come to bless our union." The radiance of a rainbow surrounded them, and seemed to have the effect of softening the hearts of all within reach of its rays—for not only did the face of the Fairy assume its wonted **gentleness,** but repentant tears bedewed the

cheeks even of the intruders. Then Randolph
fell at the Fairy's feet to intercede for these
creatures, in which prayer he was joined by the
princess. At the same moment the dragons
were transformed into a flock of doves, the
Fairy's sign of truce. She then opened her
arms to Randolph, and tenderly embraced him.
"Son of my heart," said she, "nobly hast thou
withstood this last temptation, for it was intended
only as another trial of your virtue. Had you
taken advantage of my offer to wreak vengeance
upon your enemies, you would have been again
stained with sin. Live hereafter in peace and
happiness, and know that your fallen country
will yet arise from her ashes in greater glory

than ever. She has suffered, but she is purified, and thus prepared for greater blessings than before. And you," said she, looking severely at the uninvited guests, "you may well rejoice that your captor, being a Confederate soldier, spurns to trample on fallen foes, even though they be the pillagers and plunderers of his own household. Repent your ways while you have time. A respite of punishment has been granted to enable you to return and warn your people against Nemesis, whose uplifted hand is ready to strike the blow that will carry destruction in its wake. Tell them to unshackle the race of heroes they have enslaved, that their temple of liberty may not be shattered and sow terror in their midst. Tell them to restore ill-gotten goods, and bring content to the sad hearts and plenty to the scanty boards of those whom they have ruined. Retribution's sword, sharper than that of Mars, is suspended over them. Go avert the evil before it is too late." Gracefully waving her wand, a number of gorgeous and magnificent balloons appeared, in which the explorers gladly departed in the midst of the acclamations and rejoicings of the inhabitants of the moon.

When last heard from the party had landed at the Central Park; but instead of trying to convert their erring people, were making large fortunes by carrying lovers beyond the clouds, to be united in the bonds of matrimony.* They

---

*The writer is a witness to the fact that a bridal party in New York, the summer of 1865, had their marriage celebrated in a baloon during its ascent.

have never again undertaken to invade the moon, but there is no knowing what may yet take place, as they are a very indefatigable people.

FINIS